Contents

Published by Pedigree Books Limited
Beech Hill House, Walnut Gardens, Exeter, Devon EX4 4DH.
E-mail books@pedigreegroup.co.uk
Published 2006
© Chapman Entertainment Limited 2006.
Licensed by Target Entertainment.

fifi
and the Flowertots

Chapman ENTERTAINMENT

Pedigree®

COSGROVE HALL FILMS

£7.99

Say hello to the Flowertots

Hello,
I'm Fifi Forget-Me-Not.
Welcome to Forget-Me-Not Cottage!
I love living in Flowertot Garden and I am very proud of my organic garden. I can pick all my own fruit and vegetables!
There is always something exciting happening here! Later you can read about some of my adventures and have fun with my games and puzzles. But first its time to meet my friends!

Bumble

Bumble lives in Honeysuckle House and he is my very best friend! He is always happy and ready for fun. Bumble loves going on exciting adventures with me – even though he's a little bit accident-prone and suffers from hayfever!

Pip

Pip is a very young Flowertot. He loves helping out around the garden and he is always full of excitement! Sometimes he gets into trouble when he believes Stingo's silly stories, but we love Pip just the way he is!

Webby

Webby is older than the rest of us and she is very, very wise. All the Flowertots go to Webby for advice. She's very good at explaining things and she knows the answer to every question!

Violet

Violet is the youngest Flowertot of all. She is very calm and quiet, and she loves painting. She lives in Flowertot Cottage with Primrose. They are best friends but sometimes they fall out and argue!

Primrose

Primrose hates anything messy. She can't understand why I like gardening because it makes me so dirty! She makes all her own clothes and sometimes she makes pretty things for her friends, too!

Poppy

Poppy is loud and friendly – and sometimes a little bit bossy! She loves sports and is very down to earth. Poppy runs the market stall and sells delicious, sweet-smelling food to all the Flowertots.

Aunt Tulip

Aunt Tulip is everybody's favourite aunt! She is very friendly and kind, and she can always make me laugh! We love her and her pet Grubby, and she gives some of the best tea parties in the Flowertot Garden!

Stingo

Stingo is the garden pest. He thinks he is better than us just because he is older! He watches us from high up in Apple Tree House and he enjoys causing trouble. Stingo loves to boss poor Slugsy about!

Slugsy

Slugsy is Stingo's only real friend. He is just as naughty as Stingo, but he often ruins Stingo's cunning plans by accident! Slugsy sometimes bursts into song, which really annoys Stingo! Slugsy is very fond of Primrose.

Flowertot Babysitter

Fifi Forget-Me-Not was getting ready for a very exciting day.
She was going to look after Aunt Tulip's pet, Grubby.
Grubby couldn't talk. He could only squeak.
He squeaked when he was happy.
He squeaked when he was sad.
And he squeaked very loudly when he was hungry!

10

Fifi opened the oven and pulled out the biscuits she had baked.
Just then Aunt Tulip and Grubby arrived.
"Hello darlin'!" said Aunt Tulip. She put Grubby down on the floor.
"Hi Aunt Tulip, hi Grubby!" said Fifi. "I've made lots of yummy Flowertot biscuits!"

Grubby jumped into Fifi's arms and squeaked. But Aunt Tulip shook her head.
"Oh no," she said. "Grubby can't have anything to eat today! He's going to have grub-bake and custard later. I don't want him to spoil his tea by snacking all day."

11

Aunt Tulip said goodbye to Grubby. But Fifi was very worried.
"Buttercups and Daisies!" she said. "How am I going to take Grubby's mind off food?"
Fifi took Grubby out into the garden to show him her compost heap.

Fifi began to rake up leaves to add to the compost heap. But then she saw that
Grubby was eating the compost! "No, stop that!" cried Fifi. She picked Grubby
up and he squeaked crossly. "I'm sorry," she said. "But remember what Aunt
Tulip said. No snacking!"

Just then, Fifi's friend Pip arrived. "Hi, Fifi! Hi Grubby!" he said. "I'm going to Violet's house for blackberry pie. Do you want to come?" "I can't, Pip," sighed Fifi. "And Grubby can't either. We've got to do some deliveries for Poppy."

Fifi whistled for Mo. "Come on, Grubby," she said. "Let's fill up Mo's drum with compost. It's the only way to make Mo go!" But while Fifi was filling Mo's drum with compost, Grubby crept away!

Pip, Violet and Primrose were enjoying their blackberry pie when Grubby arrived!
"Grubby! I thought you were helping Fifi!" cried Pip. "I'm going to take you back."
"Oh, let him have a piece of pie with us first!" said Violet.
So Primrose gave Grubby a piece of pie and he gobbled it up.

Fifi was very happy when Pip brought Grubby back! "Naughty Grubby!" she said.
"You mustn't run off!" "I'm going home to make my own pie," said Pip.
Grubby wanted to go with Pip. But Fifi said no.
 "Poppy's waiting for us," she told him. "Let's go, Mo!"

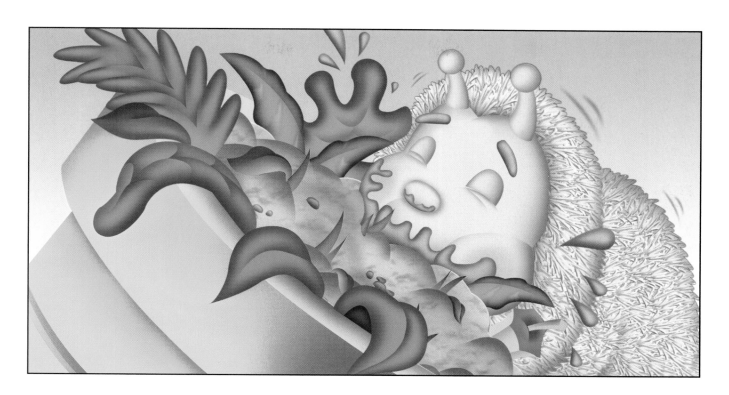

Fifi's first delivery was to Violet and Primrose's house. "Stay right where you are, Grubby," she said. "I won't be long." Fifi knocked on the door. But while she wasn't looking, Grubby started to eat the compost again!

When Fifi came back, Grubby hid behind Mo's trailer. "Where's Grubby?" gasped Fifi. "He's gone! Oh no! I've got to find him!" Fifi jumped into Mo, but he wouldn't start! "Mo's empty!" Fifi cried. "But I've only just filled him up!" "Don't worry," said Violet. "I've got a bucket of potato peelings. You can use those!"

As soon as Mo was filled up with potato peelings, Fifi drove off to look for Grubby. She didn't know that he was still hiding on the back of Mo! "Pip said he was going to make a pie," Fifi said to herself. "I bet greedy Grubby's at Pip's."

Fifi went to Pip's house to check. But Grubby wasn't there!
"I'd better go back home and see if he's there," sighed Fifi. "Let's go, Mo!"
But Mo wouldn't start! Fifi went to check the potato peelings. They were all gone!

Luckily Pip had some gooseberry leaves to fill up Mo's compost drum.
Fifi drove home as fast as she could. "What am I going to tell Aunt Tulip?" she
sniffed. But when Fifi got home, Aunt Tulip spotted Grubby in the drum!
"Come on darlin', let's go home for tea," she said.

Grubby shook his head. Then Fifi looked in the compost drum. Suddenly she
understood! "Grubby's been eating Mo's compost all day!" she cried.

Chocolate Crispy Cakes

Try my recipe for delicious chocolate crispy cakes!

Ingredients:

A big bar of chocolate

A box of cornflakes

Cake cases

1 tablespoon of golden syrup

2 tablespoons of butter

1 tablespoon of drinking chocolate

Tools:

A saucepan

Cake cases

A baking tray

A tablespoon

A wooden spoon

A grown-up to help you

18

What to do:

1. Lay the paper cases out on a baking tray.

2. Break the chocolate into pieces.

3. Put the pieces into a saucepan.

4. Add the golden syrup, butter and drinking chocolate.

5. Ask a grown-up to help you melt the chocolate.

6. Keep stirring with a wooden spoon until all the butter and chocolate has melted.

7. Mix the cornflakes into the chocolate to make a stiff mixture. Remember to stir carefully so the cornflakes don't break up!

8. Put a large spoonful of the mixture into each cake case.

9. Put the paper cases into the fridge for an hour.

10. Eat your cornflake cakes!

Pip The Explorer!

Pip has been exploring Flowertot Garden on his scooter. But now he is lost! Can you help him find his way to Flowertot Cottage ?

Flowertot Cottage

Flowertot Friends

Aunt Tulip and Grubby have come to visit Fifi!
Use your crayons to copy the colours onto the picture at the bottom of the page.

Pip The Gardener

Fifi and Bumble were playing outside when it started to rain.
They had to rush inside and wait for the rain to pass.
"Oh, Fiddly Flowerpetals!" said Fifi. "I've got so much to do in the garden today!"
Bumble was standing next to the window.

22

"Look, Fifi!" he cried. "The sun's come out again!"
Fifi ran outside happily. Now she could get to work in her garden again!

Later that day, Fifi looked around her garden.
She had been working very hard.
"The flowers are polished, the beans are
weeded and the new flower bed has
been dug," she said
with a smile. "All
done, Bumble!"

Pip was watching Fifi and Bumble.
"Oh, I wish I had a garden like Fifi's," he thought.
"I'd grow lots and lots of things. I'd be Pip the Gardener!"
Just then, Bumble noticed a bare patch of earth. "Er, Fifi…" he said, pointing to
the bare patch. "**Oh, Fiddly Flowerpetals**, I forgot about the baby lettuces!" said
Fifi. "They need feeding – we had better go and get some compost."

23

Just as Fifi and Bumble were about to leave, Pip jumped over the fence.
  "Fifi!" he called. "Fifi, will you help me?"
   "What's the matter, Pip?" Fifi asked.
   "I want a garden just like yours," he said, looking at the bare patch of earth.
   "Can I have this bit? Please?""All right, Pip," chuckled Fifi. "You can plant anything you want here. This can be your garden."
   Pip was very excited!"We're going to get compost for the baby lettuces," said Fifi.
"See you later!"She drove off in Mo and Bumble followed her. Pip looked at his little patch of earth.
"Now, what shall I grow?" he wondered.

When Fifi and Bumble arrived to collect some more compost, they got a shock. Almost all the compost was gone!

"Diddly Dandelions!" groaned Fifi. "I was going to fill it up last week and I, er..." "Forgot!" Bumble laughed.

"ME, forget?" said Fifi with a chuckle. "Impossible!"

"Don't worry, Fifi," said Bumble.

"There's enough here for your lettuces. Afterwards we can go and collect scraps from everyone to make more compost."

Fifi and Bumble filled up two little baskets with compost and then turned to go home.

When Fifi and Bumble got back to
Forget-Me-Not Cottage,
Pip was standing by his little
garden. It was full of flowers!
"Finished!" he said.
"That was quick!" gasped Fifi.
Then she looked at the flowers.
"Pip, those look just like…"
"Fifi's flowers!" finished Bumble.

"Oh, Pip," Fifi groaned.
"You can't pick flowers I've
already grown!
Plants don't grow like that.
Without roots they'll wilt and
die." Pip was shocked.
"Why don't we help you plant
something else?"
said Fifi, kindly.
"Let's go and get my seed box."

26

Fifi went through her seed box with Pip.

"Carrots?" said Fifi.

"Too long," Pip replied.

"Buttercups?" said Bumble.

"Too yellow," Pip said, shaking his head.

"How about cress?" said Fifi.

"What's that?" asked Pip. "It's a kind of salad that's very easy to grow," Fifi explained. "And you can eat the cress afterwards," added Bumble.

Pip gave a big smile. "Cress, yes!" he said with a grin.

"A cress garden! Brilliant, thanks Fifi!" Pip took the packet of cress seeds. He ran out of the house and over to his garden. He sowed his seeds. Then he sat down to wait.

When Fifi and Bumble came out to put the compost on the lettuces,
they saw Pip sitting by his garden. He looked very unhappy.
"What's wrong?" asked Fifi.
"The seeds don't work!" Pip cried. "I've waited for ages and nothing happened!"
"Plants take longer to grow then that," chuckled Fifi. "You have to wait for the seed
to open and make roots and leaves."
"Golly Gooseberries," said Pip.
"Gardening takes longer then I thought!"
"Maybe if you had something else
to do, it would help you wait
for the seeds to grow," said
Bumble.
"I know!" cried Fifi.
"You can help us collect
scraps to make more
compost!
You can tell everyone about
your cress garden at the same
time!"

28

Pip worked hard
collecting compost from
all his friends.
He invited them all to
come and have cress
salad with him.

Violet and Primrose
promised to come. Poppy
said that she would be
there.
Pip even visited Stingo.

Stingo gave him a piece of
old bread.
"I suppose we can spare this
old bread," said Stingo.
"But what do we get in
return?"
"Come and have lunch,"
said Pip.
"I'm growing cress."
Pip worked hard all day until
Fifi had lots of compost.
"Now let's go and pick my
cress!" said Pip.
"Pip!" cried Fifi.
But Pip wasn't listening!

29

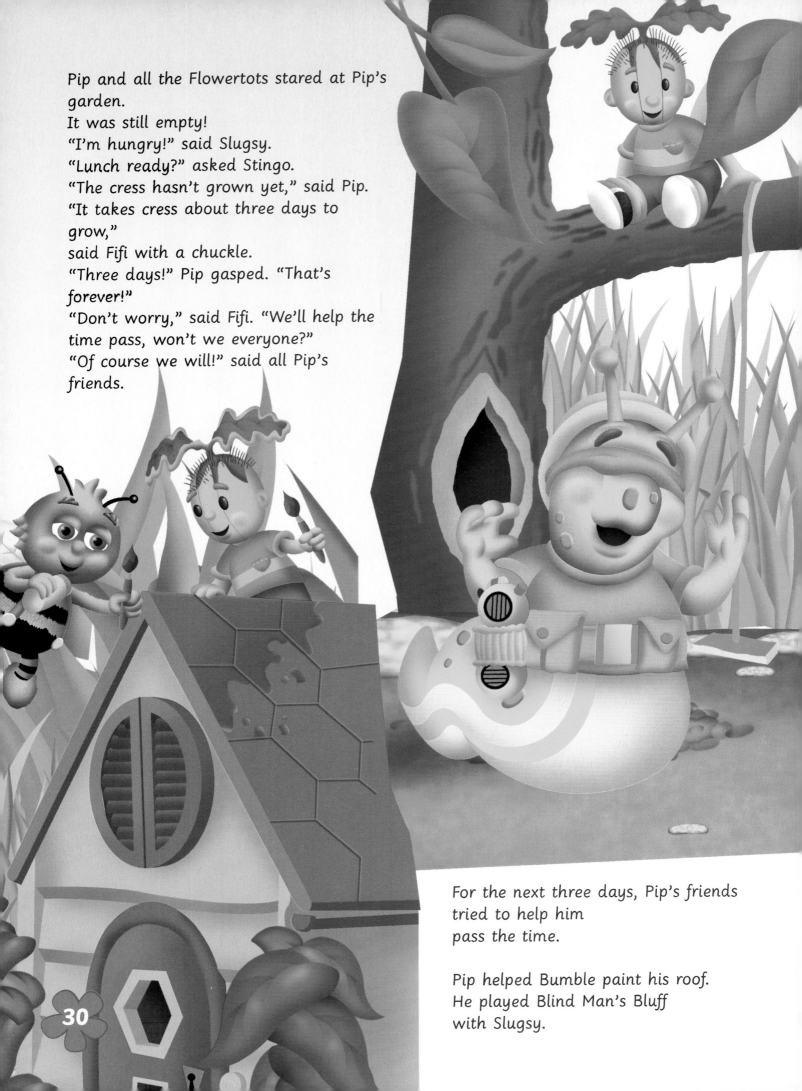

Pip and all the Flowertots stared at Pip's garden.
It was still empty!
"I'm hungry!" said Slugsy.
"Lunch ready?" asked Stingo.
"The cress hasn't grown yet," said Pip.
"It takes cress about three days to grow,"
said Fifi with a chuckle.
"Three days!" Pip gasped. "That's forever!"
"Don't worry," said Fifi. "We'll help the time pass, won't we everyone?"
"Of course we will!" said all Pip's friends.

For the next three days, Pip's friends tried to help him
pass the time.

Pip helped Bumble paint his roof.
He played Blind Man's Bluff
with Slugsy.

30

At last the cress was ready!

"Look!" Pip shouted. "Look, I grew this! ME! I'm a gardener!"

"Who's going to cut it down?" asked Primrose.

"What do you mean, cut it down?" cried Pip.

"That's what you do with cress," said Bumble.

"You cut it and put it into sandwiches."

"No, it's mine," cried Pip. "I don't want to cut it!"

"But what are we going to eat?" asked Stingo.

"I know!" said Bumble. He ran off and picked two lettuces from Fifi's garden.

"Enough salad for everyone!" he said.

And they all tucked in!

Pip's Guide to Growing

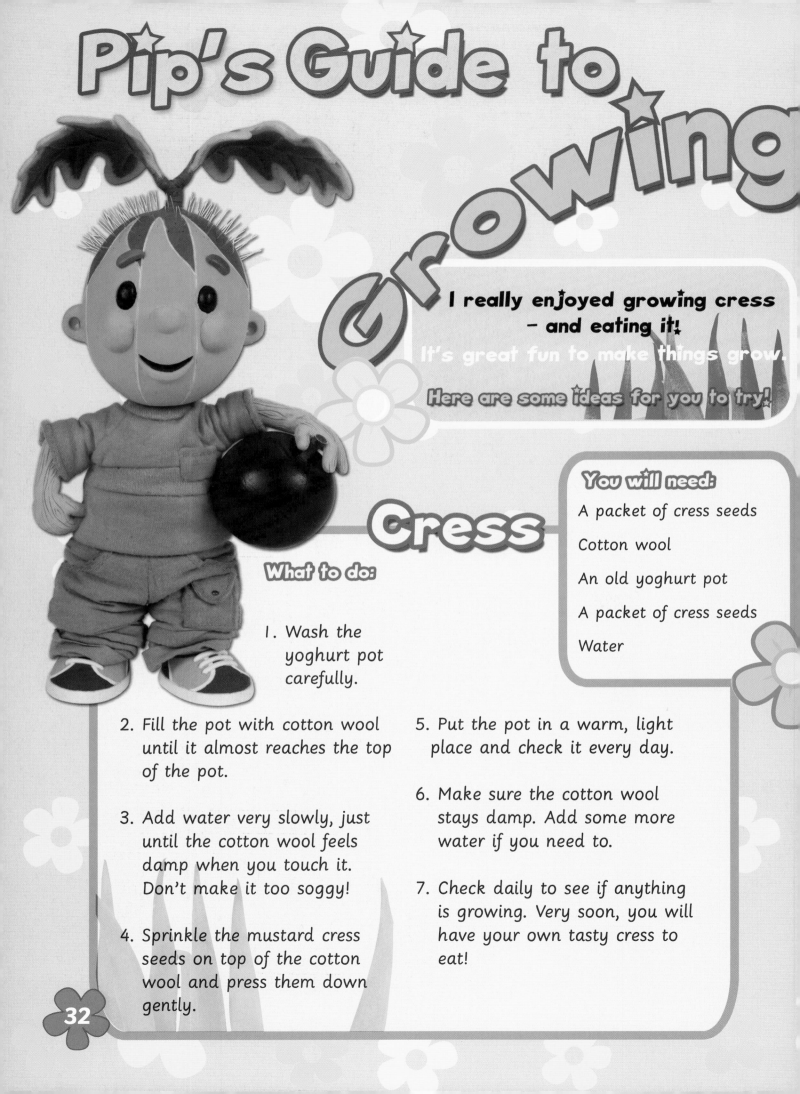

I really enjoyed growing cress – and eating it!

It's great fun to make things grow.

Here are some ideas for you to try!

Cress

What to do:

1. Wash the yoghurt pot carefully.

2. Fill the pot with cotton wool until it almost reaches the top of the pot.

3. Add water very slowly, just until the cotton wool feels damp when you touch it. Don't make it too soggy!

4. Sprinkle the mustard cress seeds on top of the cotton wool and press them down gently.

5. Put the pot in a warm, light place and check it every day.

6. Make sure the cotton wool stays damp. Add some more water if you need to.

7. Check daily to see if anything is growing. Very soon, you will have your own tasty cress to eat!

You will need:

A packet of cress seeds

Cotton wool

An old yoghurt pot

A packet of cress seeds

Water

Carrot Tops

You will need:

A carrot

A saucer

Water

A grown-up to help you

What to do:

1. Choose a carrot that has a little shoot on top.

2. Ask a grown-up to help you slice about the top of the carrot off.

3. Put the carrot top on a saucer with a little bit of water in it.

4. Put the saucer on a light windowsill.

5. Top up the water every day.

6. In a few days leaves will start to grow from the top of the carrot tasty cress to eat!

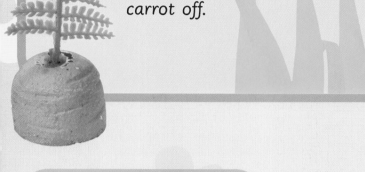

Sunflowers

You will need:

A packet of sunflower seeds

A trowel

A sunny spot in the garden where there is plenty of room

Compost

A grown-up to help you

What to do:

1. Use your trowel to dig up the soil where you are going to plant your seeds.

2. Dig in some compost.

3. Make some little mounds of earth about half a metre apart.

4. Plant about five seeds in each mound, just under the surface.

5. Water the mounds every day. Keep the earth damp until you see the seedlings!

6. When the seedlings have a few leaves, pull out the weakest ones. On each mound, leave the two best ones to grow.

7. Soon you will have lots of tall, beautiful sunflowers!

Bumble's Counting Confusion

Bumble is trying to count the jars of honey in his house. Can you help him out? How many jars of honey can you count? Write the number on the honeycomb!

34

Delivery Day!

Fifi and Mo are making some deliveries for Poppy. Look at the two pictures. Can you spot five differences between them?

The Wasp that Cried Ouch!

Pip, Bumble, Violet, Primrose and Fifi were playing Flowertot rounders.
Fifi threw the ball to Bumble and he hit it.
Fifi ran to catch it. They were having lots of fun!

The Flowertots didn't see Stingo and Slugsy hiding in the grass. Bumble was getting ready to catch the ball. But suddenly he stumbled on a stone and fell backwards! The ball hit him on the head! "Bumble is so silly," laughed Stingo.

Fifi, Pip, Primrose and Violet gathered around Bumble.
"Are you OK Bumble?" asked Primrose.
"I've hurt my elbow!" groaned Bumble.
"I think you need a bandage," said Primrose. "I'll be right back."

Soon Primrose was back with a bandage. Fifi and Violet brought Bumble
 some strawberry juice and honey flapjacks to make him feel better.
Stingo and Slugsy were still watching through the grass.
"Yummy strawberry juice and flapjacks," said Stingo.
"Maybe Bumble isn't quite so silly after all. Time for Stingo to get some goodies too!"

Soon Bumble was feeling much better. But as he thanked his friends,
they heard a strange noise. "AHHHH!" "What was that?" said Pip.
Suddenly Stingo fell out of the sky and landed on the ground next to them!
He rolled around on the ground as if he was in terrible pain.

They raced over to Stingo. "Where does it hurt?" asked Primrose.

"Everywhere!" said Stingo, pretending to sob.

"Don't worry, we'll make sure you feel better," said Bumble kindly.

The Flowertots helped Stingo home and Primrose wrapped him in lots of bandages.

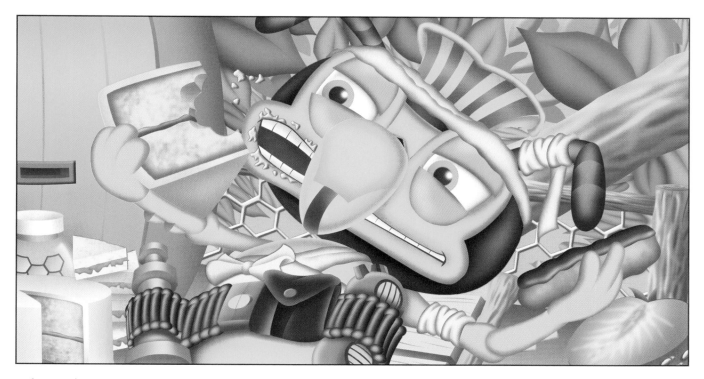

Fifi made Stingo a cranberry and apple drink. Violet picked some blueberries.
Bumble filled a pot with some yummy honey. Soon Stingo was surrounded by piles
of tasty food. "Slugsy!" he said. "Get me a banana milkshake."

"But we haven't got any bananas, boss," said Slugsy.

"WELL GO AND GET SOME!" shouted Stingo.

As soon as Slugsy had gone, Stingo jumped up from the sun lounger.
He picked up a biscuit and popped it into his mouth.
"That's better," he chuckled. "**Bingo stingo,** this is the life!"
Just then Fifi, Violet and Bumble were walking up to Stingo's house with their gifts.

"Stingo is going to love our get-well goodies," smiled Bumble.
  "Our visit is bound to cheer him up," Fifi agreed. Fifi, Violet went up to Stingo's
balcony on the lift and Bumble flew up. They saw Stingo standing up with
a drink in his hand! Yummy, being ill is the life for me!" he sang.

"Stingo!" everyone cried. "You tricked us," said Bumble.
Stingo pretended to be ill again. But Fifi, Violet and Bumble weren't fooled.
"It's too late Stingo," said Fifi. "We know you're not ill!"
"You didn't even hurt yourself, did you?" asked Violet.

Just then, Slugsy arrived with a big banana. "Boss, you can walk!" he smiled.
"You're better!" "No, Slugsy," said Fifi. "Stingo wasn't ill after all. He tricked us."
Slugsy was shocked. "You tricked me!" he said. Stingo didn't know what to say.

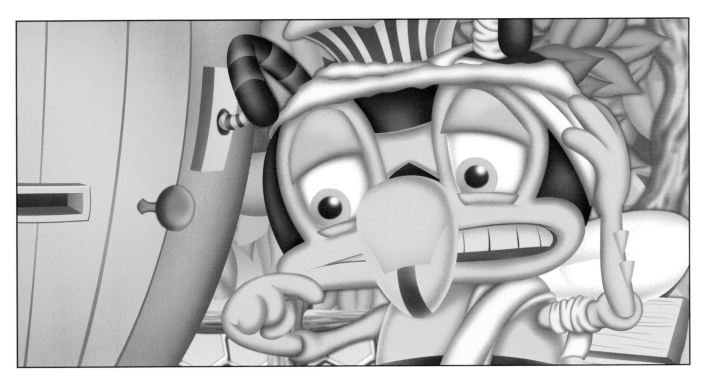

"Come on, Flowertots," said Bumble. "Stingo doesn't get any more get well goodies.
Lets go and play." "Do you want to come and play, Slugsy?" asked Fifi.
"I'd love to," said Slugsy. They left. Stingo was all alone.
"Maybe my plan wasn't so good after all," he said.

Down in the clearing, the Flowertots were playing Flowertot rounders again.
Slugsy hit a very good shot! Up on his balcony, Stingo was all by himself.
He looked at the piles of food. "At least I've got all this yummy food to keep me
company!" he chuckled.

The Flowertots were playing rounders with Slugsy when they heard a loud groan.
"It sounds like Stingo's up to his old tricks again, pretending to be ill," said Fifi.
"I'd better check up on him, just in case," said Slugsy.
Fifi handed Bumble the bat. I'll come with you," she said.

When they arrived at Stingo's house, he was lying on his sun lounger.
"Ouch," he cried. "My tummy!" Fifi looked around at all the empty plates.
"Stingo has eaten so much that this time he really IS ill," she said.
 "But don't worry, he'll soon feel better. Maybe he'll think twice next time before crying ouch!"

Violet's Flowertot Pen Pot

I love art and making things! I'm going to show you how to turn an old flowerpot into a perfect pen holder!

What you will need:

A small flowerpot

Cardboard.

Some old jeans or denim

material

Sticky tape

Scissors

Glue

Brush
Light blue ribbon

Yellow ribbon

A grown-up to help you

1 Make sure the flowerpot is nice and clean. Scrub it in some soapy water and dry it with a tea towel.

2 Copy the picture of Fifi on th opposite page and colour it in.

What to do:

3 Ask a grown-up to help you cut out a piece of cardboard. It should be wide enough and long enough to go around the pot.

4 Now ask a grown-up to help you cut a piece out of the denim material, exactly the same size as the cardboard.

5 Use sticky tape to fix the cardboard around the pot.

6 Brush glue all over the cardboard.

7 Carefully cover the cardboard with the denim material.

8 Ask a grown-up to help you cut the blue and yellow ribbons so they are just long enough to go around the top and bottom of the pot.

9 Brush a little bit of glue onto the blue ribbon and stick it around the top of the pot.

10 Brush a little bit of glue onto the yellow ribbon and stick it around the bottom of the pot.

11 Finally, glue your picture of Fifi onto the front of the pot and leave the glue to dry.

12 Now you have your very own Fifi Forget-Me Not pen pot!

45

Which Stingo?

Stingo is playing a trick on the Flowertots!
He has taken lots of pictures of himself and put them all around the garden. But the real Stingo looks different to the pictures.
Help the Flowertots by finding the odd Stingo out!

46

Webby's Word Web

Lots of things are stuck in Webby's Web! Can you tell her what they are?

Point to the word that belongs to each picture.
Now use your pencil to follow the dotted lines and make the words!

**Flower   Apple
Carrot   Blueberry**

Flower
Apple
Carrot
Blueberry

47

Flying Lessons

Fifi and Bumble were
outside Fifi's house.
They were chasing a butterfly.
"I love butterflies," panted Fifi. "I'll catch it!" cried
Bumble, flying into the air. But Bumble missed the butterfly and fell on his
nose! Fifi laughed and the butterfly escaped. Not far away, in Apple Tree
House,
Stingo was on his balcony. "Slugsy!" he called.
Down on the ground, Slugsy slid towards the lift to take him up
to Stingo's balcony. "Hurry up, Slugsy!" called Stingo.

48

Slugsy was in
the lift.
He was taking a very
long time. Suddenly, Stingo
lost his temper. "I haven't got time
to wait around all day!" he said. "It's time
I did something about it! I'm off!" He flew away just
as Slugsy arrived on the balcony. "You can't go without
me!" Slugsy cried. He slid down the chute and landed on the ground
again. "Stingo?" he called. "Where are you? Stingo!" But there was no reply.
"Stingo doesn't want to play with me any more," Slugsy thought sadly.

49

On Poppy's stall, Stingo was looking at
some material.
"There we are!" said Poppy.
"What do you think, Stingo?"
"I'm not too sure," he said.

Slugsy met Bumble and Fifi.
They could see that he was sad.
"What's wrong, Slugsy?" asked Fifi.
"I don't think Stingo wants to be my friend
any more," said poor Slugsy.
"But why?"
"I'm too slow," said Slugsy. "I can't keep up
with him any more and he keeps flying off
without me. If only I could fly like you, Bumble.
Then Stingo would be my friend again."

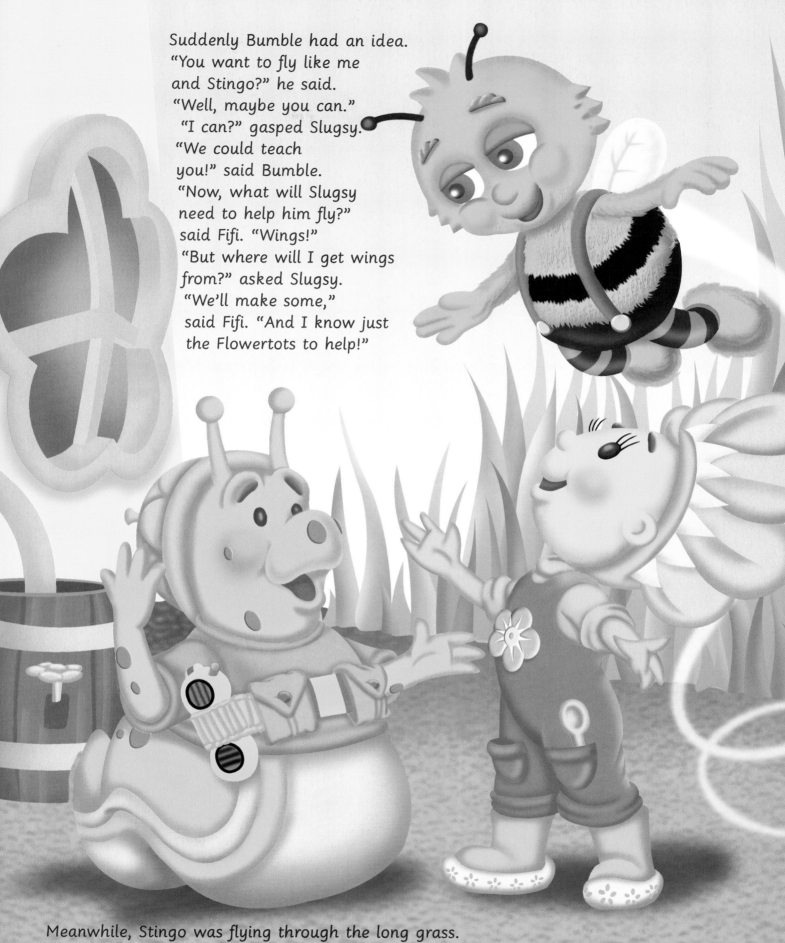

Suddenly Bumble had an idea.
"You want to fly like me
and Stingo?" he said.
"Well, maybe you can."
"I can?" gasped Slugsy.
"We could teach
you!" said Bumble.
"Now, what will Slugsy
need to help him fly?"
said Fifi. "Wings!"
"But where will I get wings
from?" asked Slugsy.
"We'll make some,"
said Fifi. "And I know just
the Flowertots to help!"

Meanwhile, Stingo was flying through the long grass.
He was carrying the material he had bought from Poppy. He landed on his
balcony.
"Phew!" he panted. "That was hard work!
Just wait until Slugsy sees what I've got for him!"

Violet and Primrose made Slugsy a pair of handmade wings made from flower petals.

"Come on, let's try them out," said Fifi.

Violet put Slugsy's new wings on his back.

"Wow!" Slugsy gasped. "They're perfect! Er... what do I now?"

"It's easy!" said Bumble. "All you have to do is flap your wings and then you'll be able to fly."

Slugsy started to flap the wings. But he stayed on the ground.

"It's not working!" he cried.

"Maybe you need a helping hand," said Fifi. "Come on, everyone!"

The Flowertots and Bumble gave Slugsy a big push.

CRUNCH!

They pushed Slugsy into a tree!

Fifi decided to try something different.
She showed Slugsy how to bounce on a trampoline.
"This feels just like flying!" she told him. "It's bound to work!"
"It doesn't look very safe," said Slugsy.
"Go on, Slugsy, it's worth a try," said Bumble.
Slugsy went up the ramp to the trampoline. He felt very worried,
but he flapped his wings and jumped.
Poor Slugsy. He wasn't very good at it!
He started to cry. "I can't!" he cried.
"I don't like it! I'm never going to be able to fly!"

53

On his balcony, Stingo was calling for Slugsy.
But there was no reply.

"Oh, **Rotten Raspberries!**" grumbled Stingo.
"Where has he got to now?
I want to show him my latest invention!"

The Flowertots and Bumble
tried to comfort Slugsy.
"Come on, Slugsy,"
said Bumble.
"You can't give up now!"
"Yes, I can," said Slugsy.
"I'm hopeless. No wonder
Stingo doesn't want to be
my friend."
"We still want to be your
friend," said Fifi.
"But Stingo was my best
friend!" sobbed Slugsy.

54

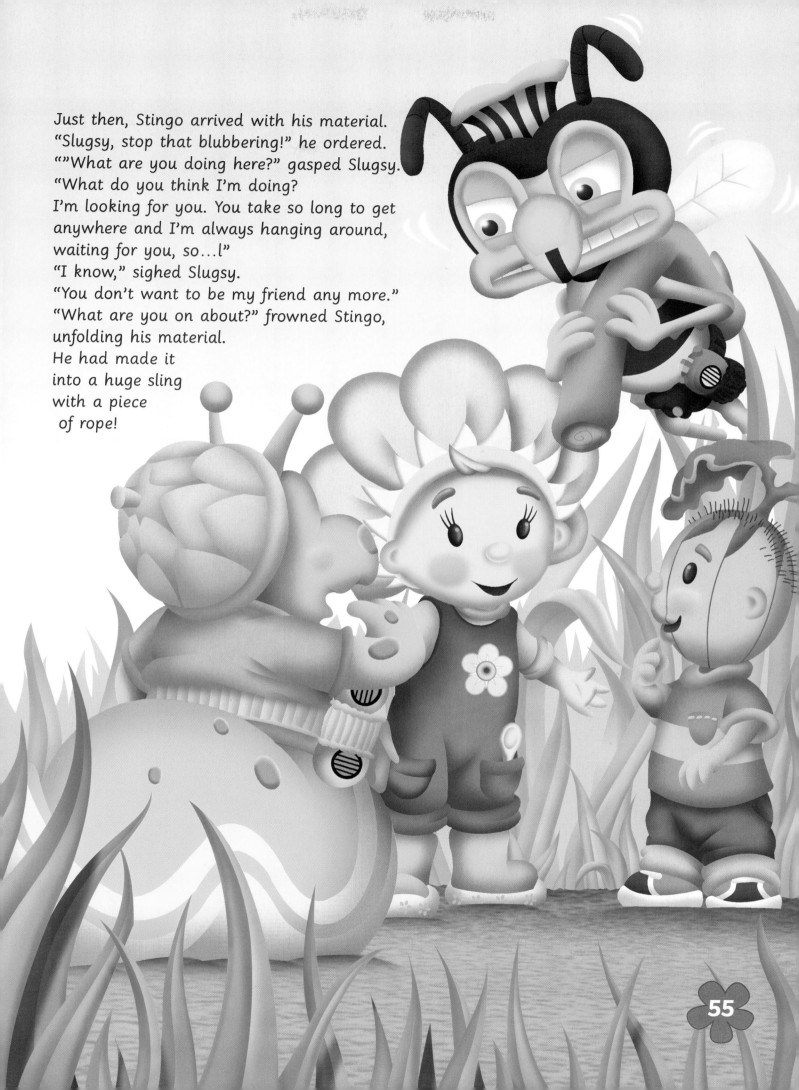

Just then, Stingo arrived with his material.
"Slugsy, stop that blubbering!" he ordered.
""What are you doing here?" gasped Slugsy.
"What do you think I'm doing?
I'm looking for you. You take so long to get
anywhere and I'm always hanging around,
waiting for you, so…l"
"I know," sighed Slugsy.
"You don't want to be my friend any more."
"What are you on about?" frowned Stingo,
unfolding his material.
He had made it
into a huge sling
with a piece
of rope!

55

"All I do is tie the rope around me," Stingo explained.

"Then you sit on the material and you'll be able to fly when I fly."

"You did all this... for me?" gasped Slugsy.

"No, you silly slug," said Stingo. "I made it so that I wouldn't have to hang around for you all day!"

Slugsy got into the sling and Stingo flew upwards.

Slugsy covered his eyes.

"What's wrong now?" asked Stingo.

"I don't like it!" cried Slugsy.

"Get me down! I think I'm gonna be sick."

"Sick?" gasped Stingo.

"Time for an emergency landing! Hold on tight, Slugsy!"

The Flowertots watched as Slugsy and Stingo
fell to the ground.
Stingo hit the ground with a thump and rolled
over onto his nose.
Slugsy landed safely.
"Are you all right, Slugsy?"
asked Primrose.
"You don't look very well,"
added Violet.

Stingo's eyes were spinning as he fell over
backwards.
"I'll be OK," said Slugsy.
"But I'm never flying again. It was horrible!"
"You poor thing!" said Primrose. "Did you hear that, Fifi?
Flying's horrible." But Fifi was sitting in the sling!
Bumble flew up and the sling liftedoff the ground.
Diddly Dandelions! Fifi Forget-Me-Not was flying!

Fifi's Garden Menu

I love eating the food I grow myself!
Here are some of my favourite garden snacks.

Menu

Scrumptious Starter
Fifi's Special Salad

———

Vegetable Treat
Crunchy Dipping Sticks

———

Scrummy Sweet
Amazing Apples

Fifi's Special Salad

What you need:

* A grown-up to help you
* Lettuce
* Tomatoes
* Celery
* Cucumber
* Red peppers
* Sweetcorn
* Olive oil
* Salt and pepper

What you do:

1. Ask a grown-up to help you chop the vegetables up.

2. Mix the vegetables together in a salad bowl.

3. Mix a few drops of olive oil into the salad and stir well.

4. Add a little salt and pepper.

5. Serve with crusty bread!

58

Crunchy Dipping Sticks

What you need:

* Carrots
* Celery
* Hummus, salsa, sour cream or any of your favourite dips
* A large plate
* Some little bowls
* A grown-up

What you do:

1. Ask a grown-up to help you cut the carrots and celery into sticks.

2. Each stick should be about 6cm long and 1cm wide.

3. Arrange the sticks around the large plate or use them to make a fun design!

4. Put the dips into the little bowls.

5. Get crunching!

Amazing Apples

What you need:

* 1 apple
* 2 teaspoons of brown sugar
* Cinnamon
* A bowl
* A grown-up

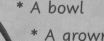

What you do:

1. Ask a grown-up to help you peel the apple and cut it into small pieces.

2. Put the pieces of apple into a mixing bowl.

3. Add the brown sugar and mix it in until all the apple is covered.

4. Put the apple into a dessert dish.

5. Sprinkle cinnamon over the top and serve!

Slugs Can't Fly!

Slugsy lost his shadow while he was trying to fly!

Look at the picture of Slugsy and match him to his shadow.

Who's Visiting?

Someone has come to visit Fifi. Join the dots to find out who it is. This character will also need some extra dots adding to her shirt and shoes. Then colour in the picture!

Fun at The Fair!

Bumble had some very exciting news to tell Fifi.

"We're having a Flowertot funfair!" he buzzed.

"We've got all our own rides and stalls and everything!"

"I love funfairs!" cried Fifi. "But I haven't got a stall or a ride for anyone to try!"

"I'm sure you'll think of something," said Bumble.

Pip and Bumble's stall was a big board with pictures of Stingo and Slugsy on it. Their faces were missing! Pip handed Fifi a wet sponge.
Pip and Bumble poked their faces through the holes! Fifi threw the sponge but it missed. Then Aunt Tulip threw a sponge and hit Pip in the face!

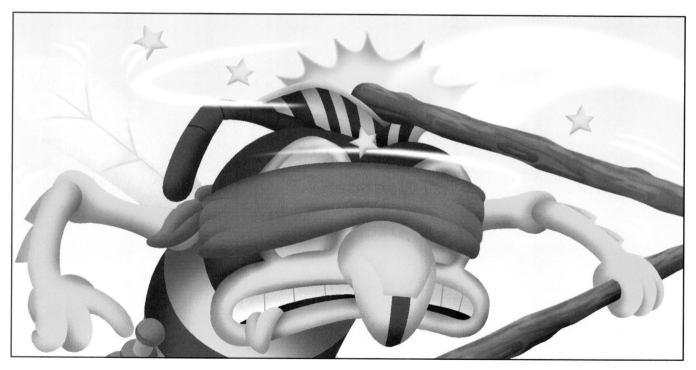

Poppy's stand was a lucky dip. Fifi had to unhook a gift from the tree with her stick. She won a big, juicy blackberry! "Well done, Fifi!" smiled Poppy.
Stingo and Slugsy had a go too, but they got their sticks hooked up with each other. Slugsy's stick hit Stingo on the head!

63

Next Fifi went to see Stingo and Slugsy's ride.

"This ride is going to scare the petals off the Flowertots!" chuckled Stingo.

"Would you like to try out our fairground ride, Fifi?" "What does it do?" asked Fifi.

"It's very gentle and very slow," said Stingo. "In that case, why not?" agreed Fifi.

Fifi stepped onto the ride and Slugsy moved the lever that sent the ride into the air.
He pulled the lever back and made Fifi stop at the top of Stingo's tree house.
Then he made the ride drop towards the ground!
Fifi's ride flew up and down through the air!

At last the ride landed with a bump and Fifi staggered off.
"That ride was so scary!" gasped Fifi. "I loved it!
I'll have to tell Primrose and Violet all about it." Fifi ran off and Stingo frowned.
"She wasn't supposed to enjoy it! We'll have to think of another way to scare them."

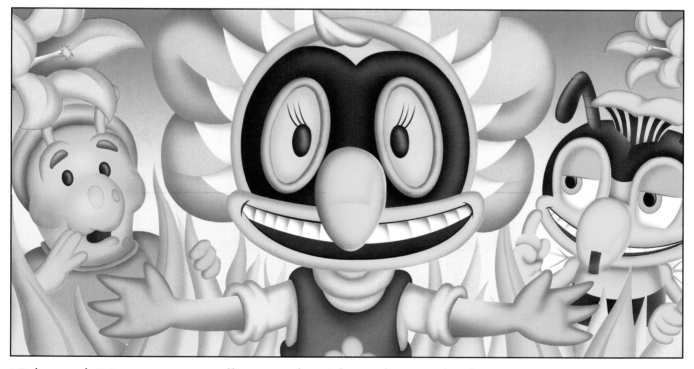

Violet and Primrose were selling masks. Fifi tried a mask of Stingo!
Stingo and Slugsy were watching from behind some grass.
"Primrose and Violet have just given me an idea," said Stingo.
"I know just the thing to scare the Flowertots, but we'll need Mo's help."

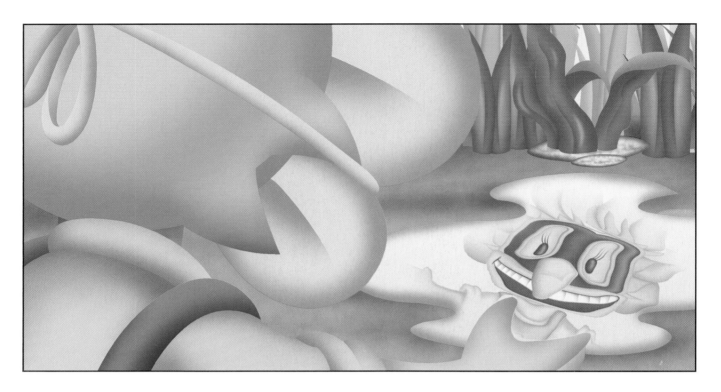

"You do look funny!" giggled Violet, looking at Fifi in the Stingo mask.
Fifi looked down at a puddle. "I can see my reflection in the puddle!" she smiled.
"It's just like a... oh, **Fiddly Flowerpetals!** What is it called? It's shiny!"

"Jewellery?" suggested Primrose. "No," said Fifi.
"It's silvery and you can see your face in it." "A bowl?" said Violet.
She handed Fifi a silver bowl. Fifi's reflection looked very funny in it!
"No. it's a mirror!" said Fifi.
"The bowl has given me an idea! I know what I can do at the fair!"

66

Stingo and Slugsy went to find Mo. "Stay there, Mo!" Stingo ordered. "We've got an important job for you." Slugsy and Stingo put on some scary masks and frightening costumes. "Welcome to Stingo's terrifying train ride!" cried Stingo.

Pip found Fifi building something. "What are you doing?" he asked.
"I'm making my very own hall of mirrors," Fifi explained. "These are special mirrors! Come and take a look." Pip saw a strange refection of himself in the mirror!
"I look all funny!" he chuckled.

Violet and Primrose were standing by the train ride. "I don't like scary rides," said Violet. "Don't worry," said Primrose. "Fifi said it was fun!"
They both jumped into Mo and the ghost train started. Stingo and Slugsy leapt around in their costumes, making scary noises. But Violet and Primrose just giggled!

"Fifi was right," smiled Violet at the end of the ride. "That was great fun!"
Slugsy and Stingo ran after them. "That wasn't supposed to happen,"
puffed Stingo. "We've got to try again!" They jumped out in front of the Flowertots.
"BOO!" shouted Stingo. Violet and Primrose screamed and ran away!

Slugsy and Stingo crept into Fifi's hall of mirrors. Suddenly they saw their reflections in the mirrors. They thought they were monsters! "Scary monsters!" yelled Slugsy. "AHHHH!" They pulled off their masks and hid behind the wet sponge board with the drawings of them on it!

"Let's check if the coast's clear, Slugsy!" whispered Stingo.
They put their heads through the holes, and... ... WHAM!
 They were hit in the face with wet sponges!
All the Flowertots were standing in front of the board! "Serves you two right for trying to scare Primrose and Violet!" laughed Fifi.

Fair Flowertots!

Fifi and her friends are having great fun at the Flowertot Fair. It looks like Slugsy and Stingo are going to get wet!

Use your crayons to colour in this picture of Fifi's friends. Try to match the colours from the picture on the opposite page!

70

Primrose's Colour Code

Primrose likes to keep Flowertot Cottage tidy.
She has told Violet to tidy up!

The pink things are going on the shelf.
The blue things are going in the box.
The yellow things are going in the cupboard.

Can you help Violet? Draw lines with your pencil to
show her where everything should go.

YELLOW

BLUE

PINK

Hole Lot of Fun!

One morning, Fifi went over to Bumble's house to help him pick some peas.
When she arrived, Bumble was struggling with a pea.
"Phew, this is a tough one!" he puffed.
"Let me help you," said Fifi. She stood behind Bumble and they
 pulled at the pea together.
They pulled very hard. The pea came off and Bumble
tumbled backwards, holding the pea!
"That's one way of doing it!" chuckled Fifi.

Not far away, Slugsy was playing explorers.
"Brave ssSlugsy explores the jungle!" cried Slugsy.
"Watch out for the giant bugsss, bosss!" "I'm bored,"
grumbled Stingo. "Nothing ever happens round here!"

Bumble and Fifi picked lots of peas and then Fifi nearly fell into a hole!
Bumble saved her just in time. "Thanks, Bumble," gasped Fifi. She knew where that
hole had come from. But she couldn't quite remember the word!
"It was made by...oh **Fiddly Flowerpetals**... they're long and wriggly!"
she said "Spaghetti?" asked Bumble. "No," chuckled Fifi.
"They live under the earth! It sounds likes germs!"
"Germs?" said Bumble."Oh, you mean worms!"
"That's it, worms!" said Fifi.
"This is a worm hole!"
"Fifi Forget-Me-Not, forgot!"
laughed Bumble.
"And I've forgotten something else!"
gasped Fifi.
"Aunt Tulip is coming round to
make oat biscuits!
Bye, Bumble!"

75

Bumble was looking at his peas when Stingo and Slugsy came along.
Slugsy knocked one of the peas with his stick and it rolled down the hole!
"Hey, mind my peas!" cried Bumble. "Sssorry Bumble," said Slugsy.
"You have just given me a brilliant idea, Slugsy!" said Stingo. "Let's have a hit-the-pea-in-the-hole competition! The winner will get a prize – and that will be me since it was my idea!"

"What's the prize?" asked Bumble.
"That is where you come in," said Stingo.
"Tell the Tots about the competition and fix up some goodies!" "And what will you do?" asked Bumble.
"We are going to organise the game!"
said Stingo.

76

At Forget-Me-Not Cottage, Fifi and Aunt Tulip were making biscuits.
"My mother taught me to make oat biscuits using her special recipe," Aunt Tulip said.
"The secret is to shake the flour extra well."
Grubby was covered in flower and he started to sneeze.
"Sorry Grubby!" chuckled Aunt Tulip. Just then, Bumble flew into Fifi's kitchen.
"Fifi," said Bumble, "we're going to have a hit the pea in the hole competition!"
"A what?" said Fifi.
"It was Stingo's idea," said Bumble. He explained about the worm hole
and the peas.

"Stingo?" asked Aunt Tulip. "Are you sure he isn't up to something?"
"That's what I thought," said Bumble. "But it seems like a good idea. Anyone can enter." **"Diddly Dandelions!"** said Fifi. "It sounds great! I can't wait!"
"Stingo says I need to find a prize for the winner," said Bumble.
"What about my oat biscuits?" said Aunt Tulip.
"We're making plenty."
"Brilliant!" said Fifi.
"Maybe Violet can make some medals too!"
"I'll go and ask her," said Bumble. He flew off as Fifi and Aunt Tulip finished making the biscuits.

78

At Flowertot Cottage,
Bumble explained about
the competition.
He asked Violet to make
some medals.
Violet smiled at Bumble.
"Yes, I'll help," she promised.
"Buttercups and Daisies!"
said Primrose. "That sounds
like fun! I'm going to enter!"

Stingo and Slugsy were
setting up the competition.
Slugsy gave some golf
clubs to Stingo.
"Good work," said Stingo.
"I'll have the thick one to
make it easier to win!"
"Bosss, are you going to
cheat?" Slugsy asked.
"No Slugsy, I'm going to
win fair and square,"
said Stingo.
"What if you don't win?"
Slugsy went on.
"Then I'll cheat!"
chuckled Stingo.

Soon all the Flowertots were gathered in a clearing
in the garden.

"Wow!" gasped Violet.

"It's like an obstacle course!" said Fifi.

"Everyone needs a stick," said Stingo.
Slugsy handed sticks out to Bumble,
Fifi and Primrose. Webby had a notepad and pencil
to take scores.

"The rules are easy," said Stingo.

"You choose a leaf shape and then use the stick to hit
the pea into the hole.
Whoever takes the fewest number of hits
is the winner and Judge Webby will count them."

All the Flowertots nodded. "Lets begin,"
said Stingo, "and may the best wasp... um,
I mean the best Tot win!"

Primrose was first to take a shot.
She hit the pea, which hit the flower and bounced off.
It flew backwards and hit Bumble on the head!
Slugsy chuckled and threw Primrose another pea.
This time Primrose hit the ball through the hole on the
flower. The Flowertots cheered. Primrose lined up another
shot. The pea stopped by the edge of the hole.
Primrose took a small putt and knocked the
pea into the hole. "Four!" said Webby.
She wrote Primrose's score down in her
notepad.

81

It was Fifi's turn next. She hit the ball
– into Stingo's mouth!
Slugsy took the pea out of Stingo's
mouth and threw it back to Fifi.
This time Fifi hit the pea up the
ramp. Everyone clapped!
"Well done!" called Primrose.
Fifi hit the pea into the hole with her
next go. "Three!" said Webby, writing
down Fifi's score.
It was Bumble's turn next. He took a
big swing and hit the ball up the
ramp and through the leaf hole. It
landed next to the hole!
Bumble's next shot missed and he
landed on this bottom. But the
thump made the pea roll into the
hole! "Two!" said Webby.

Now it was Stingo's turn!
He lined up his shot.
He hit the pea.
It went up the ramp... through the flower
hole... over the ground and...
IN THE HOLE!
"A hole in one!" cried Webby.
"Stingo's the winner!"

Stingo was over the moon!
"Sting-a-ling!" he shouted.
"I actually won fair and
square!" "No you didn't",
laughed Fifi. "You won fair...
and circle!"
Violet gave out the medals
and Aunt Tulip gave out
her oat biscuits.
"You can have a whole
lot of fun when you
play nicely with your
friends!" said Fifi.

Aunt Tulip's Hide "n" Seek

Grubby has been very greedy today! Aunt Tulip has hidden all her goodies to stop him eating any more. But, **Buttercups and Daisies**, Aunt Tulip has forgotten where she hid them all!

Can you help Aunt Tulip find her food? Each time you find something, colour in one flower!

84

Poppy's Strawberry Smoothie

This is my favourite drink – I'm sure you'll love it too!

What you need:

5 large strawberries

6oz strawberry ice cream

4 oz lemonade

2 teaspoons of sugar

A grown-up to help you

What you do:

1. Ask a grown-up to help you put all the ingredients into a blender.

2. Blend the ingredients until the mixture is thick and smooth.

3. Pour the mixture into a tall glass.

4. Serve with a colourful straw!

Stingo's Word Game

Sting-a-ling! From high up in Apple Tree House I can spy on the Flowertots through my telescope! Can you guess whose house I am looking at today?

Match the words to the pictures. Then copy the words by following the dots with your pencil!

Mo

Mo

flowerpot

flowerpot

watering can

watering can

spade

spade

87

Sports Day

Fifi was in her garden, trailing a plant up a stick.
Pip ran up to say hello.

"Hello Fifi!" he said. "What are you doing?"
"I'm sticking canes into the ground to help the
plants stand up," Fifi explained.
"I don't need canes to stand
up!" chuckled Pip. "I can
run and jump and
everything!"

88

"Have you tried the high jump?" asked Fifi.
"It's a game to see who can jump the highest." "That sounds like fun!" said Pip.
"There are lots of other fun things too," said Fifi. "I know! Why don't we have
our very own sports day?" "With prizes for the winners!" agreed Pip.

Pip and Fifi didn't know that Stingo was spying on them!
"Prizes?" he said. "Time to get fit, Slugsy!
"Er. Yes boss!" he said, as he fell off his leaf.
"Fifi's having a sports day and we're going to win!" Stingo told him.

89

Fifi and Pip started to make a hurdle. Bumble, Violet and Primrose were watching them. "What are you making?" asked Bumble.
"It's a high jump," said Fifi. "We're having a sports day."
"That sounds like fun!" said Violet.

It was Pip's turn first. He ran up to the hurdle and jumped it easily! All the Flowertots cheered! It was Slugsy's turn next.
"We can do better then that!" said Stingo. Stingo pushed Slugsy forward. Slugsy slid up to the hurdle. He tried to jump, but he could hardly get off the ground!

"Never mind, Slugsy," said Fifi. "Your turn, Stingo!" Stingo took a run up and flew over the hurdle! "Hey, that's cheating!" said Pip.

"I got over the jump didn't I?" said Stingo.

"Yes, but you're supposed to jump over the pole!" said Fifi.

"That means Pip wins the high jump!"

"Now it's time for the tug of war," said Aunt Tulip.

The girls were on one side and the boys were on the other.

They tugged and they puffed. But at last the girls won!

"Rotten Raspberries!" cried Stingo. "Hooray! We won! We won!" sang the girls.

91

Next the Flowertots lined up for the sack race.
"This is my favourite!" cried Fifi.
Slugsy was still struggling to get into his sack
"What do we have to do again?" he asked.

"On your marks!" called Aunt Tulip. "Get set! GO, TOTS, GO!"
The Flowertots all jumped off from the starting line, leaving Slugsy behind.
It looked as if Bumble was going to win, but he fell over just before the finish line.
Fifi crossed the line first!

The hurdle race was next. "I'll definitely win this one," said Stingo.
"If you say so, boss," said Slugsy. "On your marks!" said Aunt Tulip. "Get set! GO!"
Stingo was in the lead, followed by Bumble, then Fifi.
Slugsy just broke all the hurdles!

Stingo fell flat on his face and Bumble crossed the finish line just in front of him.
Stingo was furious! "I don't think sports day is my thing," said Slugsy.
"Everyone is good at something," said Fifi. "Not me," sighed Slugsy.

The next event was the egg-and-spoon race.
"On your marks!" shouted Aunt Tulip. "Get set! GO TOTS GO!"
Slugsy tripped and his egg landed on top of Stingo! Slugsy made a run for it
and Stingo chased after him. "Come back here, you slimy slug!" he shouted.

Primrose, Fifi, Violet and Pip decided to run the race again – without eggs this time.
Suddenly Primrose tripped up and started to fall.
But as Slugsy was being chased by Stingo, he caught Primrose!
Stingo tripped over Slugsy and landed on the finish line!

94

"Slugsy, you're a hero!" said Primrose. She gave him a kiss and he went very red!
"Wow, Stingo," said Violet. "You were going so fast, you beat us all!"
"But it's Slugsy who should get the praise," said Primrose.
"He caught me just before I was going to fall into that muddy puddle!"

Aunt Tulip put a medal round Slugsy's neck.
"All the winners get a medal, but Slugsy should get one too," she said.
"After all, he's the best sport!" All the Flowertots cheered. "It's not the winning that's important," said Fifi. "It's having fun and being a good sport that really matters!"

Garden Race

Start!

You will need:

A dice
A counter for each player.

How to play:

1. Throw the dice.
2. Move your counter along the board, the same number of squares as the dice you have thrown.

It is sports day in Flowertot Garden and you can join in too!

3. If you land on a flower, you can move on two spaces! If you land on some fruit, you can have another throw.

4. If you meet Slugsy or Stingo, you must go back three spaces.

5. The first one to reach the finishing post is the winner!

Finish!

Fifi's Flowertot Garden Alphabet

Fifi has been working very hard. She has made an alphabet for you, using some of the things in her garden!

Aa is for Apple

Bb is for Butterfly

Cc is for Compost

Dd is for Dandelions

Ee is for Easel

Ff is for Flowers

Gg is for Gooseberry

Hh is for Honey

Ii is for Insects

Jj is for Jasmine

Kk K is for Kite

Ll is for Lettuce

Mm is for Mushrooms

Nn is for Nests

Oo is for Organic

Pp is for Potato

Qq is for Quince

Rr is for Rake

Ss is for Strawberry

Tt is for Trowel

Uu is for Umbrella

Vv is for Violet

Ww is for Wheelbarrow

XYZ

...zzz
zzz....
Fifi is fast
asleep!

Flowertot Milkshake

Fifi was in her kitchen rolling out pastry.
She was giving a Flowertot picnic and she was making lots of yummy food.
The pastry was for a blackberry pie. There were jam tarts cooking in the oven.
Then she was going to make chocolate pancakes.

Poppy came in to Fifi's kitchen with two bottles of milk.
"Hello Fifi, I've brought your milk," she said, putting the bottles on the ground.
"Pip told me he's bringing wild strawberries to your picnic."
"He grew them himself," said Fifi. "He's very proud of them."

Poppy left and Fifi went to check her jam tarts. Just then Pip burst in to the kitchen. He knocked over the milk bottles and spilt all the milk!

"**Oh, Buttercups and Daisies,** Pip!" cried Fifi. "Be careful!"

"I came to tell you that my strawberries were ready for picking," said Pip.

"I was so excited that I didn't see the milk bottles!" "Don't worry," said Fifi.

"I can always get some more milk from Flowertot Market." "I'm so sorry!" cried Pip. Fifi hurried to the market. Poppy only had two bottles of milk left!

Later, Bumble came in to Fifi's kitchen with some fresh crunchy vegetables
for the picnic. "Thank you, Bumble," said Fifi.
 "Is there anything I can help you with?" asked Bumble.
"Could you pop over and see if Pip needs any help picking his strawberries?" said
Fifi. "Of course," said Bumble. "See you later!"
Just then, Pip was on his way to Fifi's house with a big basket of strawberries.
He bumped into Stingo and Slugsy.

"You've got some nice strawberries there!" said Stingo.
"I grew them all by myself," said Pip, proudly.

"They look deliciousss," said Slugsy. "Can I try one, please?"
Pip shook his head. "Sorry Slugsy, I'm taking them to Fifi's picnic."
"That big basket is far too heavy for you, Pip," said Stingo.
"Slugsy will take it to Fifi's house for you."
"Why me?" grumbled Slugsy.
"Because you're a big, strong, kind slug," said Stingo.
Slugsy flexed his muscles.
"This is a job for Super Slugsy!" he said.

When Bumble arrived Pip was filling another
basket with strawberries.
"Hi Pip!" said Bumble. "Fifi wants to know if you
need any help?"
"Stingo and Slugsy have already taken half of my strawberries to Fifi's house,"
said Pip. "Oh dear," said Bumble.
"I had better get over to Stingo's before it's too late."
"They wouldn't steal my strawberries, would they?" cried Pip.
"Not if I've got anything to do with it," said Bumble.

Slugsy and Stingo were scoffing the strawberries at Stingo's house.

Bumble landed next to them. "Those are Pip's strawberries!" said Bumble.

"We were... er... just on our way to Fifi's house!" lied Stingo. "We thought we'd see if the strawberries were ready for eating!"

"Fifi won't be pleased with you two," said Bumble.

105

Pip rushed into Fifi's kitchen with his basket of strawberries.

"Hi Fifi!" he panted. "I got here as fast as I could." Pip put his basket on the table and looked inside.

"Oh no!" he cried. "My strawberries are all squashed and mushy! It must have happened when I was running!"

Pip was very sad. "I've done nothing right today," he groaned.

"First I spilt your milk, then I gave strawberries to Stingo and Slugsy!"

"Stingo and Slugsy?" gasped Fifi. Pip explained what had happened.
"They said they wanted to help me," he said. "Help eat your strawberries more like!"
said Fifi. "They were very mean to you, Pip."
Bumble flew in to the kitchen. "I got what was left of the strawberries," he said.
"They're all squashed and mushy too!" cried Pip.
"Slugsy sat on them," said Bumble. "What can you do with mushy strawberries,
Fifi?" asked Pip. Fifi gave a little smile. "I've got an idea," she said.

Fifi poured some milk into her blender.
She added the mushy strawberries.
Then she put the blender on and mixed it all up
She poured it into three glasses.
"There you go Pip," she said. "A special
milkshake made from your very
own strawberries!"

"Wow, Fifi!" cried Pip. "You're
the cleverest Flowertot in
the world!"

At last all the Flowertots gathered for their picnic.
Stingo and Slugsy walked up to Fifi.
"You two aren't invited to my picnic," said Fifi.
"Oh please, Fifi!" said Stingo.
"We will be good!" added Slugsy.
"No, you're very naughty," said Fifi.
"You lied to Pip and you stole his strawberries!"

Stingo turned to Pip.
"I'm really, really, really, really sorry, Pip," he said.
"So am I," said Slugsy
That's OK," smiled Pip. "I forgive you."
"Now you've said you're sorry, you can join in!" said Fifi.
"Now, who wants a delicious wild strawberry milkshake?"